This igloo book belongs to:

....

Contents

igloobooks

Published in 2014
by Igloo Books Ltd
Cottage Farm
Sywell
NN6 0BJ
www.igloobooks.com

FIR003 0614
2 4 6 8 10 9 7 5 3
ISBN: 978-1-78197-326-4

Printed and manufactured in China
Written by Xanna Chown
Illustrated by Melanie Florian

Bedtime Stories for Princesses

igloobooks

Phoebe and the Unicorn

Princess Phoebe was very lonely. She lived in a grand palace, but had no one to play with. Then, one day, when she was playing in the palace gardens, Phoebe found a sparkly, gold bracelet. "How pretty," she said, putting it on.

Suddenly, there was a burst of sparkles and a shining unicorn appeared. Princess Phoebe was amazed. "This bracelet must be magic!" she cried.

"Hello," said the unicorn in a soft voice. "I'm Glitter. Climb on my back, and we'll go for a ride."

Glitter kneeled down and Phoebe climbed onto his back. "Hold tight," he said, then he flapped his wings and whoosh! He soared up and up into the sky until the royal palace was far below. "Wow!" cried Phoebe. "This is amazing!"

Glitter carried Phoebe up through the clouds until they reached a magical, sparkling mountain. "This is where the cloud fairies live," said the unicorn.
Then, Phoebe saw two cute little fairies that giggled and waved at her.

Phoebe and the unicorn landed on the fairy mountain.
"Hello, pretty princess," said the little fairies, fluttering their wings.
"Will you come and play with us?"
"Yes, please!" cried Phoebe and she joined in a game of catch.

It was great fun playing fairy games, but it made Princess Phoebe very hungry. So, the fairies made her a magical feast that came floating through the air. Everything was delicious, even though it was very small.

9

All too soon, it was time for Phoebe to go home. She climbed onto Glitter's back and he flew away. "Goodbye, fairies," said Phoebe, with a wave. The fairies smiled and waved back. "Come and visit soon," they said.

10

Back in the palace gardens, Phoebe said goodbye to Glitter. She was sad to see him go, but he promised to come back whenever she wore the magic bracelet. "Thank you, Glitter," said Phoebe. "Now I know I will never be lonely again!"

The Pet Party

Princess Petunia was having a royal pet party. She'd invited her friends over and told them to bring their pets. "This is going to be fun!" said Petunia to her pet kitten, Smudge, as she put up balloons on the cheery tree.

First to arrive was Princess Sapphire with her unicorn, Sparkle. "Hello, Petunia," said Sapphire. She chatted happily to her friend, but didn't notice that Sparkle was busy nibbling at the tablecloth.

Princess Twinkle arrived next and was enjoying her lemonade so much that she forgot to keep an eye on her new puppy, Wags. He started to chase Smudge round the garden, making Princess Sophia's parrot squawk and flap in alarm.

14

"This is a disaster!" cried the king, as Princess Scarlet's baby dragon accidentally set fire to a flower bed. "Nonsense," said the queen. "The animals are just hungry." She rang a little silver bell. Ding-a-ling-a-ling!

The palace doors opened and the royal cooks rushed out of the kitchen, each one carrying a silver plate. They had cat and dog food, unicorn and dragon food, even a dish with birdseed and some flies for a pet spider.

At once, the pets stopped messing around and started to eat. "Now we can enjoy our picnic," said the queen. The princesses all cheered. "This is such fun," beamed Petunia. "Let's have another pet picnic tomorrow!"

The Mermaid Princess

Princess Petal lived in a beautiful palace near the sea. One day, Petal was feeling a bit bored, so she collected stones and shells from the beach and sat down on the sand to look at them.

Suddenly, she heard a splash and turned to see a mermaid, sitting on a rock. "Hello, I'm Coral," she said. "What lovely shells and pretty stones." Princess Petal was very surprised. She had never seen a mermaid before.

"I wish I was a mermaid," said Petal.
"You can be," said Coral. "All you have to do is wear my magic necklace."
Petal put the necklace on and suddenly, she had a tail!
She dived beneath the waves with a big splash.

Coral showed Petal her underwater home. "Wow!" said Petal, as little fish darted here and there between the rocks. She saw a jiggling jellyfish and an octopus with long, waving arms.

Coral's mermaid friends came swimming by and everyone
played hide-and-seek. Petal loved swishing in and out of the
sea grass with her mermaid's tail and she loved her new
mermaid friends.

When it was time to go, Petal gave back the magic necklace and thanked Coral for a lovely day. Coral smiled and flicked her tail. "I'll see you soon, little mermaid friend!" she said and dived with a splash into the sea.

Rainbow Dress

Princess Polly was going to her first ball, but she wasn't excited. She looked at the ballgown that the royal dressmaker had made. It wasn't the sort of dress Polly liked at all. It was quite plain and Polly didn't feel like a real princess in it.

"Oh, well nevermind," sighed Polly, gazing out of the window. Suddenly, she noticed a great, big rainbow arching into the palace garden. "Can I go and find the end of it?" she asked. "Yes, but don't get your ballgown dirty," said the queen.

The princess dashed out of the door and across the lawn.
She wanted to find the end of the rainbow before it vanished.
Whoops! Gloopy mud splashed and splattered her dress as she
ran through the royal flower beds.

26

Polly raced through the apple orchard, puffing and panting, but then she stopped. There was the end of the rainbow! Sitting at the bottom was a rainbow fairy, with sparkling wings. "Hello," said the rainbow fairy. "Would you like to make a wish, little princess?"

Princess Polly looked down at her muddy dress. "I wish I had a lovely, sparkly ballgown," she said. "My mum told me not to get this one dirty! She won't be very happy."
Suddenly, there was a ZING! Polly had a sparkly, new ballgown. "Wow! Thank you," she said to the fairy and ran all the way back to the palace.

"Your dress looks beautiful," said the queen, as Princess Polly arrived at the royal palace. "It's all thanks to the rainbow fairy," said Princess Polly. "Now I know that I will look beautiful at the grand royal ball!"

The Lost Treasure

Princess Poppy lived in a crumbling castle and her clothes were full of holes. "If only we could find great-grandfather's treasure," said the queen to the king, with a sigh. "Then we'd be rich again." They didn't know that Princess Poppy was listening behind the door.

"Let's go and look for the treasure," whispered Poppy to her puppy, Patch. As they searched the tallest tower, Patch knocked over an old painting. As if by magic, the wall behind it swung away and a secret staircase appeared.

Poppy and Patch tiptoed down the twisty steps into a
dark cellar. There was an old, wooden chest in the middle of
the room, with a golden coin, a silver key and a riddle inside.
"It must be a clue!" said Poppy.

"Take the right tunnel to find the fish, then throw in the coin and make a wish," she read. Behind the chest were two tunnels, one on the left and one on the right. "We'll take the right one," Poppy said.

The tunnel was dark and dusty and Poppy was glad when they reached the end. They came out beside a fountain in the castle gardens. Water splashed out of a stone fish into a shell-shaped bowl below.

Poppy threw the gold coin into the water. "I wish to find the secret treasure," she said, excitedly. There was a magic flash, and a pretty, blue-winged fairy floated out of the fountain. "Do you have the key?" she asked.

Poppy showed her the silver key. The fairy dived down under
the water and came back with a wooden box. Poppy put the key
into the lock and it opened right away. The box was full of gold
and sparkly jewels.

Poppy and Patch rushed back to the castle. "We've found the lost treasure!" she shouted. The king and queen couldn't believe their eyes when they saw Poppy.
"Thank you, Poppy," said her dad, laughing. "I think the real treasure is you!"

Spooky Sleepover

Princess Pearl loved sleepovers, especially when she told ghost stories to her friends Amber, Opal and Jade. "There's a spooky ghost that clangs and clanks around this palace at night," she whispered. The other princesses squealed and giggled. They loved ghost stories, too.

"Let's play hide-and-seek," said Pearl, when she had finished the story. She counted to ten, while everyone hid. Pearl saw Opal's feet sticking out from behind the curtain. "Found you," she said. "Come on, let's look for the others."

Opal and Pearl crept out into the corridor. They looked under tables and behind cupboards when suddenly, "Atishoo!" someone sneezed. It was Jade. "Found you!" said Pearl and Opal. The three princesses tiptoed along quietly, looking for Amber.

40

It was quiet in the long gallery. Suddenly, there was a clanking, clanging sound. "What's that?" said Pearl, feeling scared. "Maybe it's the ghost!" whispered Opal, feeling scared, too. "Look!" cried Jade. "That suit of armour is moving!"

"It IS the ghost!" cried all the girls together. The suit of armour fell with a crash to the floor. Then, they saw Amber hiding behind it. "Sorry," she said. "I toppled the armour by mistake." Everyone giggled and ran back to Pearl's bedroom.

The princesses were very happy there was no ghost, but they still decided to eat their midnight feast with all the lights on. "We've had enough sleepover excitement for one night," said Pearl, laughing. All her friends agreed.

Princess Pansy's Pet

Princess Pansy had spent all day playing with her pet dragon, Sparkles. He was really cute and full of fun. At bath time, Sparkles even jumped into the tub with her and splashed around in the bubbles.

"Come on now, Sparkles," said Pansy. "It's time for bed."
She gave Sparkles a bowl of warm milk, then tucked him
up in his basket, but Sparkles didn't want to go to sleep.
He wanted to play and he gave a smoky snort.

Pansy read Sparkles a story and sang him a lullaby. He just snorted even more loudly and flew around excitedly, knocking pictures off the walls and making a mess. "Oh, dear," said Princess Pansy. Then, she had an idea.

The Princess climbed into bed and picked up her teddy.
"Lucky Teddy is getting a big cuddle," she said. "Would you like
one, Sparkles?" At once, Sparkles gave a snort, dived onto the
bed and snuggled up next to Princess Pansy.

Before long, Sparkles was fast asleep. He snuffled and snorted and snored. "Never mind," said Princess Pansy, smiling. "It's just what little dragons do." She put on her special, dragon-proof earmuffs and settled down. Now everyone would have a good night's sleep.